The Animal Code
by
Duncan James Oakley

For Herbie and Princess Tum-Tums xx

This is a story from Lumberjack Wood,
A tale of the Animal Neighbourhood.
It features a squirrel with the brightest red hair
and an ever so friendly,

but grizzly,

bear.

So many animals shared this abode
that they had to come up with The Animal Code.

It only consisted of one simple rule,
and everyone knew it,

they taught it at school.

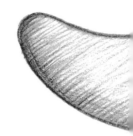

The rule was to always be good to each other,
this helped the animals all live together,
'cause if you'd like others to be nice to you,
the best way to do it is be nice to them too.

The bear and the squirrel were an unlikely team
but the pair had become quite good friends,
it would seem.
The squirrel would dance while the bear
roared with laughter

and the bear liked
having somebody
nice

to look after.

Now all of the animals liked to eat nuts
but the little red squirrel would eat far too much.
You should only eat so many nuts every day
but the squirrel ate so many

that her fur

would turn grey

(and everybody knows that grey
squirrels are so much naughtier than
the red ones!).

On one of these days, in her grey squirrel mode,
the naughty grey squirrel broke The Animal Code,
Her mischievous side got her up to no good,
and she broke the one rule of Lumberjack Wood.

She spat at the rat and she howled at the owl,
She badgered the badger and made the wolf growl,
She de-logged the frog and she goaded the toad

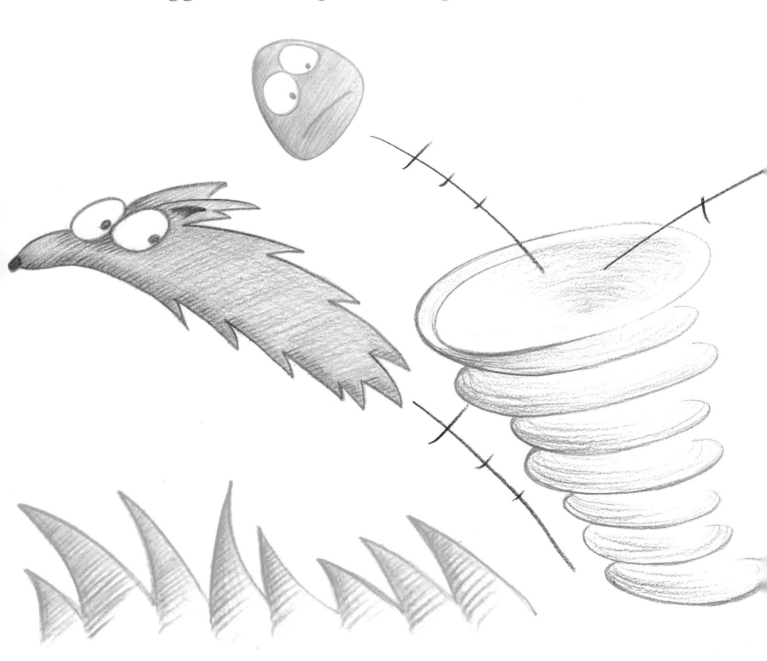

and she sent an old deer

running off

down the road.

She poked all the moles back into their holes,
then she blocked them all up with hedgehogs and voles,
She teased all the weasels, they couldn't believe her
when she nicked all the sticks

from her good friend the beaver.

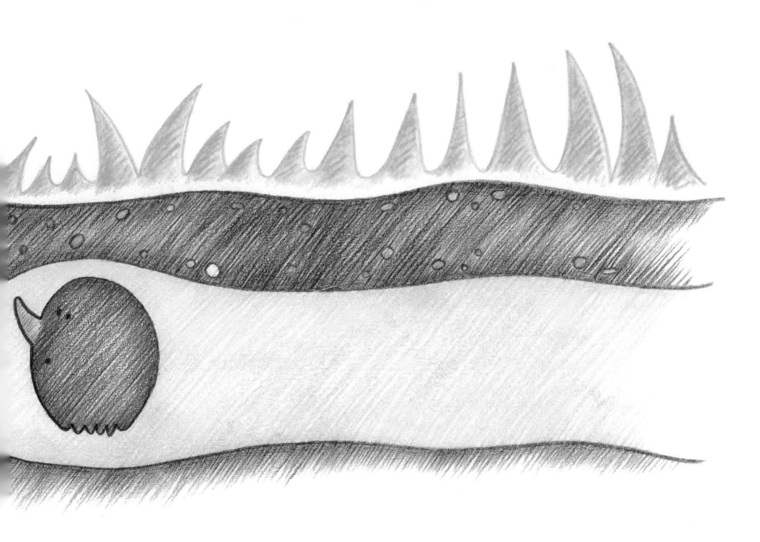

She'd shaken the snake and she'd scared off the hare
then she turned her attention to her good friend
the bear,
And as the bear slept under an old oak tree,
this was a great time for a joke,

thought she.

One hundred acorns, in an old bird's nest,
hanging from the tree, just above the bear's head,
then she jumped up and down till she fell off the branch,
and the nuts all came down in a huge avalanche!

(and everybody knows that a bear likes his sleep
and doesn't like to be woken up).

The squirrel gave the bear such a big scare
that he screamed and he roared and leapt up in the air.
The squirrel was amazed at how far the bear jumped,
as he soared through the sky and landed with a thump,

and a splat,

And the squirrel...

was flat.

And it served her right.

Don't get me wrong, the squirrel was fine,
Just a bump and a scratch, she'd got lucky this time,
But slowly her naughty grey fur became red,
and she knew there was a great deal of

"Sorry"

to be said.

The animals were all feeling under the weather,
so they set up a meeting and all got together
to discuss what to do with their naughty little friend
who ate so many nuts she would go round the bend.

And so they decided to make a decision,
Their naughty friend Squirrel must be taught a lesson,
And if that lesson was to be any good,
They'd need

           every creature

                      from Lumberjack Wood.

So the stoats in their coats, the newts in their suits,
The rats in their hats, all met in the woods.
The weasels, the ferrets, the badgers, the moles,
the reindeer, the beavers, the ants and the voles,

The snake and the woodpecker, Owl and the frog,
The wolf and the skunk and every hedgehog,
The hare, the fox, the bear and a mouse,
All stood together at the naughty squirrel's house

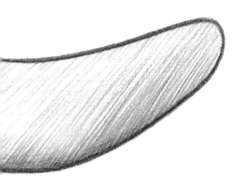

Then every single animal and every tiny bug,
Surrounded the squirrel for a big group hug,
'cause if you'd like others to be nice to you,
the best way to do it is be nice to them too.

Printed in Great Britain
by Amazon